WEE LITTLE
CHICK

By Lauren Thompson
Illustrated by John Butler

Simon & Schuster Books for Young Readers
New York   London   Toronto   Sydney

It was spring in the
barnyard and the
wee little chick was
all brand-new.

This wee little chick
was the littlest little chick.

"My, you're so tiny!"
bleated the nanny goat tall.

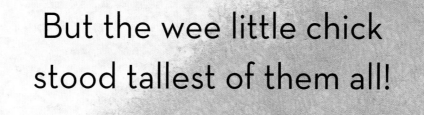

But the wee little chick
stood tallest of them all!

"Such a tiny little peep!"
squealed the plump piglet pink.

But the wee little chick
peeped loudest of them all!

"Such tiny little legs!"
gaggled the giggly goosey goose.

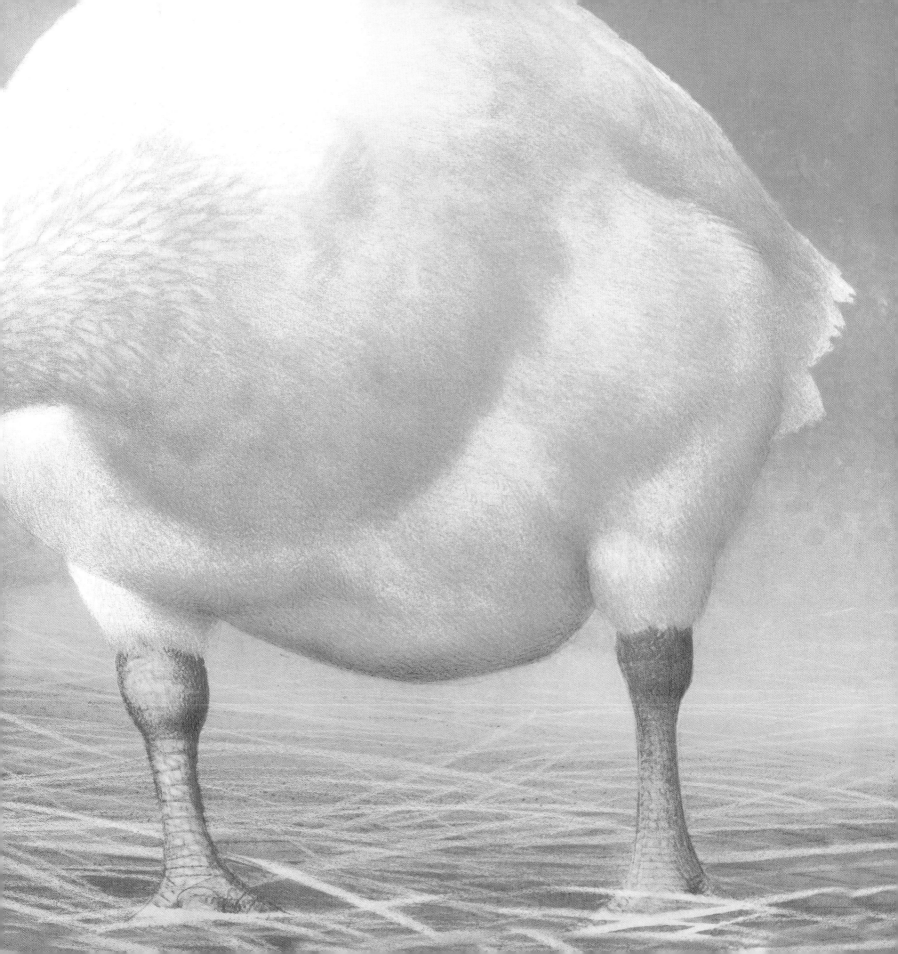

But the wee little chick
ran fastest of them all!

"Such a tiny little beak!"
mooed the wobbly bobbly calf.

But the wee little chick
found the biggest seed of all!

Then Mama Hen clucked,
"Tut, tut, tut!
She's my wee little chick
and she's just big enough!"

Oh, that wee little chick
was such a proud little chick!

Then the wee little chick
and all the little chicks
snuggled close to Mama
for a wee little sleep.

Sweet dreams!

To Charlotte—L. T.
For Cath—J. B.

SIMON & SCHUSTER BOOKS FOR YOUNG READERS
An imprint of Simon & Schuster Children's Publishing Division
1230 Avenue of the Americas, New York, New York 10020
Text copyright © 2008 by Lauren Thompson
Illustrations copyright © 2008 by John Butler
Book design by Lucy Ruth Cummins
The text for this book is set in Neutra Text.
The illustrations for this book are rendered in acrylic paint and colored pencils.
Manufactured in the United States of America
2 4 6 8 10 9 7 5 3
Thompson, Lauren.
Wee little chick / Lauren Thompson ; illustrated by John Butler.—1st ed.
p. cm.
Summary: When the other barnyard animals comment on how tiny the littlest chick is, the proud
little one peeps louder, stands taller, and runs faster than any of them.
ISBN-13: 978-1-4169-3468-4
ISBN-10: 1-4169-3468-5
[1. Size—Fiction. 2. Self-confidence—Fiction. 3. Chickens—Fiction. 4. Animals—Infancy—Fiction. 5. Domestic animals—Fiction.]
I. Butler, John, 1952- ill. II. Title.
PZ7.T37163Wee 2008
[E]—dc22
2007016411
0412 LAK